T0128741

The Journal *of* Anthony Medina

Anthony Medina

Order this book online at www.trafford.com
or email orders@trafford.com

Most Trafford titles are also available at major online book retailers.

Print information available on the last page.

ISBN: 978-1-4907-9367-2 (sc)
ISBN: 978-1-4907-9371-9 (e)

Trafford rev. 02/07/2019

www.trafford.com

North America & international
toll-free: 1 888 232 4444 (USA & Canada)
fax: 812 355 4082

Contents

The Story of Chess

Thesis

This is a purely fictional story there is almost no truth behind it at all so it is with great privilege to write this story. This was written with all intense to be a children's bed time story after all everything has a story. I tried not to worry so much about the beginning I did, but I tried worrying more about the ending and it was not so much peoples flaws as it was about there strengths. Although the game changes a little bit each time the inventor changes some would say that I've written this so that God will show his love towards British people others would say that it was coincidental that I wrote this tale. It was in medieval times when Chess was invented. I asked myself "where was Chess invented" After searching a globe I've decided in Buckingham Britannia England mainly because that rhymed the best. Looking at a Chess board I said to myself "what were these pieces in history" and it's not just what these pieces were it's also was what these pieces looked like. In this tale Courtney invented the Chest game although she titled the game Chest like a treasure Chest Courtney developing most of the game not all of it she would of wanted the game to of been a Childs game tragically Courtney died before finishing the game. But her brother Bucky would buy rights to the game developing more of the game and leaving more information behind the game was to be titled Chess sadly enough Bucky died shortly after a battle due to the negligence of the British leaders, Courtney and Bucky leaving behind a Dad Mom and three Sisters and three Brothers. Since the game was getting great remarks, the British would work together and buy rights to the Chess game after many problems, the British would invent a game that people would enjoy for years and years.

"Who invented chess?" the British of course

"Where was chess invented?" Surely it originated in London where all things fowl of Brittan England emerge but it was invented in Buckingham Brittan England

Introduction

(Narrator)

It was about the second century in Britannia England while Britannia was at war with Scotland expanding the Roman kingdom. There was a King Edward and a Queen Elizabeth who dwelled in a castle in Buckingham. There was many military there was a Navy that protected the boarders of ocean. Knights, who were the leaders of the military and would compete in events called jousting, there were Soldiers who kept the peace. Also Jesters used for entertainment usual entertainment was plays that many people would go to watch. A usual thing for most people to do was to get an artist to draw a portrait of them. There were many hard working Men and Women Peasants. It was said that a few yards of silk turned a Peasant into a Noblemen, it was also said that a few yards of silk turned a Peasant into a Queen. But for an unfortunate family it was just the beginning.

The Story of the Origin of Chess

(Narrator)

T he oldest of eight children Courtney aside from her work and household duties was inventing a game and not just any game the game was to represent a family and coming from the Gibbs family a large ten member household herself it seemed right to be crafting this game. Courtney sitting at a table across from her oldest brother Bucky talking about her invention (Courtney) Chest was intended to be a child's game similar to playing with dolls, the game is to be titled Chest like a treasure Chest I'm not to sure of the strategist of the game yet other then the game has sixty four squares, and a symbol of the British flag going thru the board, the symbol of the British flag was like see thru and put there to be patriotic, and both opponents have sixteen pieces. The second row of pieces being the Children) the two end pieces being the Bankers (Accountants,) first row second pieces in being the Jesters) the Horse being the Guards for the pieces of Dad and Mom) the pieces of the Dad being the Guardian) the pieces of the Mom being the second Guardian. (Narrator) Of course these pieces were quality selected because most normal families have a Dad and Mom and Children, like all animals they become territorial and the Horse being the guard animal, families are usually mayhem so you need Jesters, you also need somebody to budget money like Bankers (Accountant.) The mother Kieran had to pick up supplies and since Britannia was at war with Scotland it was very dangerous at the time. So Kieran said to Courtney. (Kieran) stay inside until I get back. (Narrator) But she didn't listen Courtney was stabbed to death by Dia so unfortunately Courtney was not able to finish inventing Chest. Nine years would pass since the tragic death of Courtney.

The Story of the Invention of Chess

(Narrator)

Chess would change hands from the original inventor and would be invented by a man it was Bucky the brother remembering looking back towards his life when Bucky was younger. Courtney would harass Bucky by calling him names like stupid or dumb also Courtney would do cruel things to Bucky by making him wear funny clothing like tight and bright cloths in hopes to build him tougher. Bucky never being wise enough at the time to tell Courtney he had though she was depressed and or had a mood disorder. Bucky grieved and sadden by his sister death though to him self all his emotions of anger and rage changed to loving and caring and thought you're my sister I still care about you anyway so he went at the age of twenty thru the legal system and got rights to the game Chest. Bucky was drafted off to war somewhere in Scotland near the front lines while not in combat Bucky would occupy his time with inventing Chess. Bucky died from a treatable disease so unfortunately Bucky was not able to finish the game due to the negligence of the British leaders the leaders of the military instead of putting supplies into soldiers kept the money and spent it into themselves. This is what information they found in his pack which was taking back to his Dad and Mom, six remanding Siblings. Chess was supposed to resemble the British kingdom and the members who occupied it. The game is to be titled Chess; the game is with sixty four squares, and a symbol of the British flag going thru the board, and both opponents with sixteen pieces. Square two and square seven the second row being the Soldiers, the first row square h and square a being the bankers (Accountants,) the square g and the square b being the Jesters, square f and square c the Horse being the Guards for the King and Queen, square d and square e the pieces of the King being the Ruler, square e and square d the pieces of the Queen being the second Ruler. Bucky selected these pieces because what a military has is a King Queen Guards Soldier's, war is sad so you need Jesters, and you need somebody to pay these servants like Bankers (Accountants.) Six months would pass since the death of Bucky.

The Story of Chess

(Narrator)

Aside from daily duties Out of fear of losing the game Chess to Turtle Island also of sadness for Courtney and Bucky the British would buy rights to the game Chess so Chess would change hands again the British inventing the game. The board and pieces were meant to resemble a battle field also the importance of the characters in the field. The British men talking amongst themselves said. (British Men) You know it is said that women are smarter then men perhaps they are or perhaps there not (Narrator) so the British men named the game Chess because it was supposed to be a sexist joke if you say Chess fast enough it sounds like Chest. The British Men and Women gathering and talking to each other saying, (British Men and Women) You know I always wanted to laugh at something ignorant but just not talk to it let's name the piece of Horse a Knight, (Narrator) so the piece Horse was named a Knight it was supposed to be a racist joke. While they where inventing the game they let some people try the game just as an experiment. So Wanda was playing Chess with Maurice the male being easy to manipulate and naïve at his age (Wanda) the piece Jester looks more like a Bishop (Maurice) agreed and said sure (Narrator) so because of that distracting rude comment the British named the pieces of Jester a Bishop. The British, talking amongst themselves, said (British Men and Women) the King and the Queen of Buckingham do nothing more then make laws all day. Wouldn't it be funny to change placement of the pieces Knight and of the pieces Bishop to make the King and Queen angry maybe they will change them back. (Narrator) Unfortunately that never happened so the British ended up with pieces that did not make sense strategically in the game. Finally there was enough information to make the game putting the finishing touches in the game. The Chess board with sixty four squares and the colors of red white and blue going thru the board, and each opponent with sixteen pieces. Row two and row seven the pieces the Pawn being the Soldiers, square h and square a the pieces of the Rook being the bankers (Accountants,) square g and square b the pieces of the Knight being the Guards for the pieces of King and of the pieces Queen, square f and square c the pieces of the Bishop being the Religious Figure, square d and square e the pieces of King being the Ruler, square e and square d the pieces of the Queen being the second Ruler, the pieces were hand Selected because the military has a King and Queen who lead the higher ranked Soldiers, the Knight who lead the Soldiers, war is bloody so you need a Bishop, the Rook became the banker (Accountant) because there skills matched job description. So the British finally invented the game Chess which people would enjoy for years and years to come.

Page eight

Ending

(King Edward)

S o the world still turns then as it does now and people are still humans and make mistakes (Queen Elizabeth) of course. (Narrator) So King Edward and Queen Elizabeth of Buckingham ordered all the people of Britannia to have the Chess game they said (King Edward and Queen Elizabeth) it's a must have game, (Narrator) most people would agree and say Chess is an interesting game, the remanding members of the Gibbs family the Dad and Mom also the three Sisters and three Brothers where granted royalties from the Chess game the eight of them became Nobles and like others they held well played Chess games for years and years. You know nobody knows what became of the Noble family other then they're wealthy and still live in Britain somewhere. Chess would be a popular game and like all good things that must come to an end story became legend and legend turned to memory and memory faded away until now British Chess medieval times the end.

Writer Anthony Medina

"Why and or what I write this story?" so that I would like it and people would like it as well that and I would of wrote this story a long time ago but I didn't know how to well that and I don't remember any more

Notes

(Narrator) It was really interesting writing this story because this story has its sense of conspiracy. Truthfully the game Chess is boring because it doesn't make enough sense. Now picture this board with sixty four squares being the battle field, both opponents with eight Pawns, two Rooks, two Bishops, two Knights, and a King and a Queen. The thing that doesn't make sense is if the Knight were a Human Knight the placement of the Knight makes no sense either if you were to change placement of the Bishop and Knight that would make better sense. The Bishop is a Religious Figure, so the Bishops has no place in a battle field if the Bishop could be an Archer, The Rook is somebody who has a lot to do with gambling the Rook has no place in a battle field if the Rook were cavalry you know Men over Horses. So stick with me I'm not trying to repeat myself the movement of the pieces would be the same the characters would change. The board with sixty four squares, both opponents with eight Pawns the Pawns being the soldiers, two Cavalry, two Archers, two Human Knights, a King, and a Queen. The game would make better sense I think thanks for reading bye.

Special Thanks

I would like to thank Maureen Grape for taking time to read my story and for her honest and tuff criticism. I would like to thank Ian Shaffer for taking time to read some of the different variations of my story. I would like to thank Barb Keener for reading some of the earlier versions of my story and for her inspiration. I would like to thank Pastor Conrad Kanagy for taking time to read my story. I would like to thank Wallina Garner for taking time to read some of the different versions of my story and for her inspiration. I would like to thank Bobbie from the adult literacy council for taking time to read my story and for helping me edit my story. I would like to thank Jackie Kissel for taking time to read one of the earlier versions of my story and for her inspiration. I would like to thank my Mom Carmen Medina for taking time to read some of the different versions of my story and for reading my story. I would like to thank my Sister Melody Martinez for inspiring me to write children stories and for taking time to read some of the different versions of my story. I would like to thank my Brother William Medina for taking time to read some of the different versions of my story and for his inspiration. I would like to thank any one else who may of read my story or who may of helped with my story.

Writer Anthony Medina
Writer Anthony Richard Medina
Writer Anthony Richard Old English (Dick) Medina Arabic (Holy City)

The Story of
Black and White

Thesis

(Narrator)

In the early twenty first century a billon air named Andy called a meeting with the leaders of the k-k-k and the Black Panthers. Before Andy arrived at the meeting Brandon of the K-K-K also Sean of the Black Panthers were in a room not enjoying each others company. So Andy arrives late he pulls a chair closer to the African and the lightly skinned person Andy says "I need one of each of your best trained men." "So that I can use them for an experiment" Brandon and Sean said "what kind of experiment" Andy explaining "I want to place the both of them in an abandon city that I own." "If they both hate each other then they'll probably kill each other right." Andy asked Brandon "who do you think would kill who?" Brandon said "I think my white will kill the African." Then Andy asked Sean "who do you think will kill who?" Sean said "I think my African will kill the white." Andy said joking "I bet you one hundred thousand dollars each that neither of them will kill each other" Brandon said "I'll take your bet I have a man named Kurt." Sean said "I'll take your bet to I have a man named Jimi" without hesitation at the expense of Andy Kurt and Jimi where dropped of at different corners of the sealed abandoned city. Kurt, being raised in a middle class K-K-K family not really liking Africans because of his background, Jimi growing up in a middle class Black Panther family not really liking or associating with light skinned people because of his background, months would pass before the either of them would notice that someone else was there although the next few months seemed like years. Kurt and Jimi would run into each other inevitable when Kurt finally ran into Jimi Kurt's first reaction toward Jimi was "slap me in my face so that I know that you're real" so Jimi "slapped Kurt." Jimis first reaction to Kurt was the same "slap me in my face to let me no that you're real" so Kurt "slapped Jimi." After a few days of living in the same house in different rooms Kurt and Jimi would talk to each other mainly it was just them yelling in an ignorant rage at each other. Kurt, finding new reasons for hating Africans, also Jimi the same, finding new ways for hating light skinned people, one day while Kurt was talking to Jimi, Kurt saying "the reason I hate African people is because they smell and because there brown, Kurt still saying, God must have been in a bad mood when he made African people." Jimi saying "how many wars did white people start a lot" Jimi still commenting "how many wars did Asian people start few" Jimi talking "how many wars did Hispanic people start few." Occasionally Kurt and Jimi would fight kicking the piss into each other usually Kurt would win but Jimi would never let Kurt just hit him. Kurt one day in an angry rage threw milk over the face of Jimi, Kurt said "that's the closest you'll ever get to being white." Like I said Kurt would win most of there fights but not that fight. Months and months would pass bye the both of them doing things as if they were in repeat. So never the less Kurt was telling Jimi the reason he hates African people. Kurt saying "all of this time I've been telling you my problem and this whole time you've been calming me

down," Jimi saying "I know" so more months and months and even years would pass Kurt saying to Jimi "when I die I'm going long before you" Kurt never telling Jimi the reason he said that. The reason was because Kurt "didn't want to lonely" so eventually Kurt died; A few days would pass until the death of Jimi.

Introduction

(Narrator)

It is early in the twenty first century while the corrupted government argues amongst themselves the economy is broken. It is not uncommon for someone use the government. Many Americans drive lighter more fuel efficient vehicles. Also many people have flat screen televisions. Where cell phones are a necessity, the internet is easy excess to knowledge. Being born any class of there's little chance of going up or down.

Body

(Narrator)

It is early in the twenty first century. Andy a million air who succeeded in wealth and fame, Andy that doesn't get tired of filling his days with adventure. Andy called a meeting with one of the leaders of the K-K-K and one of the leaders of the Black Panthers. So the meeting is set, the meeting is to take place in a rented office space. Brandon a leader of the K-K-K arrived early. Sean a leader of the black panthers arrived early as well. Brandon and Sean started arguing not in loud voices but you could tell they were angry. Brandon complaining "about the negativity in rap," Sean complaining "about the negativity in rock." Of course the two of them were not enjoying each others company. Finally Andy arrives a couple of minutes late after Andy arrives he pulls a chair closer to Brandon and Sean. Andy said (Andy) "I need one of each of your best trained men." Naturally Brandon and Sean asked (Brandon and Sean) "what for?" Andy said (Andy) "it's for an experiment of mine." Brandon asked "what kind of experiment?" Sean asked the same. Andy said (Andy) "I want to place them in an abandoned city of mine. Andy said (Andy) "if they both hate each other then they'll try to kill each other right." Andy asked Brandon (Andy) "who do you think will kill who?" Brandon replied (Brandon) "I think the white will kill the African." Andy asked Sean (Andy) "who do you think will kill who?" Sean replied (Sean) "I think the African will kill the white." Andy said Brandon joking (Andy) "I bet you one hundred thousand dollars that they won't kill each other." Brandon said (Brandon) "I have a man named Kurt, and I'll take your bet." Andy said to Sean still joking (Andy) "I bet you one hundred thousand dollar's that either of them won't kill each other." Sean said (Sean) "I have a man Jimi, and I'll take your bet" (Narrator) so the deal is set. The next day Kurt was dropped off by helicopter. In a Sealed abandoned city. Jimi was dropped off by helicopter soon after at the opposite side of the city. Kurt's first plan of action was to find shelter, Kurt stayed in a near by house. Jimi found shelter as well, Jimi would stay in a near by house, both of them learning quickly that the electricity worked but there was no television or radio. But there was plenty of d-v-d-s and c-d-s to use. Kurt usually would grab caned food to eat, Kurt used a near by field to harvest food. Kurt aside from daily duties would watch d-v-d-s and listen to music, and occasionally exploring. Jimi would get caned food the same from a local store, Jimi used a near by field to harvest food. Jimi aside from his daily routine would watch d-v-d-s and listen to music months and months would pass. The both of them living like in repeat. Eventually Kurt went exploring later in the evening, Kurt ran into

Jimi, Kurt's first words to Jimi were (Kurt) "slap me in the face so that I know you're real" so (Jimi) "slapped Kurt." Jimi's first words to Kurt were (Jimi) "slap me in my face so that I know you're real" so "(Kurt) "slapped Jimi," aside from daily task. The two of them would meet up with each other and hangout, since there was no one else they became room mates, in a house with separate rooms. The both of them would use a near by field where they would harvest corn, potatoes, garlic, onions, etc. After Kurt and Jimi living with each other Kurt used to bare knuckle box with his friends, Jimi used to compete in boxing, so the both of them went to a near by store, they got mouth pieces and gloves. Kurt would usually win at boxing Jimi persistently never letting Kurt hit him and doing nothing. Thru parts of the day Kurt and Jimi would argue. Kurt calling Jimi (Kurt) "a nigger" and saying, (Kurt) "Jimi smelled." Jimi calling Kurt (Jimi) "a cracker" Jimi saying (Jimi) "you're the worst kind of people." Jimi still talking (Jimi) "how many wars did white people start a lot, or how many wars did Asian people start few, how many wars did Hispanic people start few." (Narrator) Kurt and Jimi living there as if they were a song stuck in repeat. Kurt and Jimi arguing one morning Kurt and Jimi both finding ways of hating each other, Kurt went and (Kurt) "got a glass of powered milk and thru it in Jimi's face, Kurt saying, that's the closest thing you'll ever get to being white," (Narrator) Jimi angry started fighting with Kurt and won, years and years would pass. Them arguing like normal Kurt finding new reasons to hate Africans, but Kurt always saying (Kurt) "when I die I'm going long before you," (Narrator) Kurt never saying the reason he said that, the reason Kurt said that is because, (Kurt thinking) he I me "didn't want to be lonely." The both of them a little over eighty now, Kurt died and Jimi buried him in the back yard, a few days later Jimi died and was destroyed.

Ending

(Narrator)

" You know Kurt and Jimi never really hated each other, although they never told that to each other, mainly because of pride but they never had to, they became friends just never saying that to each other, Just to let you know were are all the same color in regards to money the end.

Writer Anthony Medina
Writer Anthony Richard Medina
Writer Anthony Richard Old English (Dick) Medina Arabic (Holy City)

The Story of
The Blacksmith
and The Princess

Thesis

(Narrator)

It was in medieval times once a long time ago there was a blacksmith, and a princess, Bill the blacksmith worked very hard for his living, making equipment for locals and weapons for the military. Bill having a normal day occupying his time with work, as Bill looked ahead his noticed a lady and not just any lady it was Anne the princess of course Bill noticed the beauty in Anne. So Bill aside from his daily duties would pay a writer to make a letter addressed to Anne. War came to Britannia so the King Edward had announced that all able body men must serve in the military. The letter was sent right before Bill was drafted. Although the princess was sent to marry a noble the noble seeing the letter before getting to the princess changed the name and who addressed it, the princess impressed by the letter married the noble. Meanwhile Bill having fought in many battles became a knight and noble blood, Bill returning home back to being a blacksmith Bill hearing of Anne being married and having children. So days would pass and months would pass and months turned into years, eventually Bill married a lady and now has kids of his own. Still leaves fall near the winter also the world still turns.

Introduction

(Narrator)

It was the second century in Britannia England, there was a King Edward, and a Queen Elizabeth. There was a navy who protected the ocean's also there were knights who were the leaders of the military the knights would compete in events called jousting. Archers who would protect castle walls or the archers were used for long range combat. There were soldiers used for keeping the peace soldiers were also used for there short ranged combat. There was blacksmith who made weapons and armor for the military also would make items for local customers. Plays were common for people to go and watch, jesters were used for entertainment. There were many hard working men and women peasants the market was for peasants who would trade and sell goods. Most people would get an artist to draw a portrait of them. Popular games were gambling or chess it was in Buckingham were a blacksmith life would change forever.

Body

(Narrator)

In Buckingham where Bill the blacksmith is working and fishing up some orders while bill was working he noticed Princess Anne, Anne occupied by soldiers, Anne was shopping at a near by market. Bill was stunned and interested by her beauty, so early the next day Bill paid a writer to write Anne. Only nobles could marry someone of the royal family but bill could care less, later in the week the letter was ready so Bill sent the letter off. King Edward had announced war with Scotland, also the first born male of every family to fight for the crown for no less then four years. Mean while the princess was set to marry William a noble of Winchester, William got word of letter and changed the name and some of its content, Anne being impressed married William right away Anne became pregnant and having children. Bill in Scotland in battle, after many battles Bill killed many enemies, the Scottish as brutal as they are, Bill was appointed Knight after taking enemy flag, after being appointed Knight bringing privilege of reading and writing also commanding military and jousting and inheritance of land, Bill survived four years of service. The knight returning to his land Bill returns to his occupation of blacksmith. Bill ashamed hears of the princess marriage and family years and years would pass. Bill met a woman and married the lady having his children, Bill learning to be content.

Ending

(Narrator)

While there where is many military, there's still many hard working men and women peasants who would still go to market. While there's always a war to be fought also money to be made by peasants Britannia didn't go to war for a while. It became a time of peace maybe things are better this way. The moral of the story is that your not always supposed to get what you because to much of a good thing is a bad thing, the end.

Writer Anthony Medina
Writer Anthony Richard Medina
Writer Anthony Richard Old English (Dick) Medina Arabic (Holy City)

The Story
The Rich Man and
The Poor Man

(Narrator)

There was a poor man and there was a very wealthy man, there was a poor man with just a few cents or just a bunch of change, the wealthy man with millions and millions of dollars. But the wealthy man needed to purchase something the wealthy man had no money with him and no way of getting money right away. So the wealthy man shouts (Wealthy Man) "for someone to loan him the money so that he can purchase an item," (Narrator) the poor man heard his shout so the poor man went over to the wealthy man and loaned him enough money. So before the wealthy man could speak, of when he would pay the poor man back, the poor man said (Poor Man) "you need not pay me back." (Narrator) The wealthy man said loudly (Wealthy Man) "why not? You know it's bad to owe dept, (Narrator) the poor man said to the rich man (Poor Man) "I'm like you." (Narrator) The wealthy man said (Wealthy Man) "how so." Narrator) The poor man said (Poor Man) "I'm wealthy in brain and mind," Narrator) so that's the ending and end of the story.

Not all wealth is money, platinum, gold, or silver.

Writer Anthony Medina
Writer Anthony Richard Medina
Writer Anthony Richard Old English (Dick) Medina Arabic (Holy City)

The Story
of The Disease
and Parasite Called
The Black Death

Thesis

(Narrator)

The disease that lived in side the parasite originated in France, a German fellow was walking somewhere near Paris, while he was walking, he accidentally walked over a parasite almost killing it. So the parasite being angry, took vengeance towards the human race, the disease and parasite didn't affect animals, the parasite and disease now in Sweden killing nearly eighty percent of the human population. The local churches appointing soldiers to find the people with the pestilence, kill them and bury them or burn them, one of the local churches appointing eighteen men, twelve close range swords men and six long range archers but the platoon needed a guide so they took one of the local monks. Heading to a near by village with few stops only to rest, the leader of the platoon temporarily went mad order two of his men to aggressively take away the weapons from a close range soldiers, stabbing him in the stomach and had him buried. But he didn't die he went into a slight coma and awoke later. At one of there resting points the now seventeen men platoon was under attack by a large band of thefts one of the thefts nearly killing an archer all of the thefts where killed one of them almost escaping with one of the platoon's horses, the leader thru a sword at his back killing him like I said almost escaping. The archer was buried although he wasn't dead He went into a slight coma and awoke later. So the now sixteen men platoon including the monk arrived at the first village looking for people with disease and parasite not finding many. The leader and his men took a break for food and wine little did they know that they were drugged?

Sleeping potion was put into there wine. They were accused of bring destruction to the village? All were killed escaped two swords men and the monks, the two remanding swords men and the monk killed nearly everybody and escaping. Word has it that the next platoon destroyed the village, killing everything years later the pestilence would vanish.

Introduction

(Narrator)

It was the second century in Sweden, there were knights who had command of the military the knights would compete in events called jousting. The archers who protected castle walls archers were used for there long range in combat. There were many soldiers who kept the peace or soldiers were used for close range combat. In this time being a blacksmith was a popular occupation. There was a bishop who appointed people duties in the religious community. The land had many hard working men and women peasants. Letters were a popular form of communication the only problem is most people didn't know how to read and write because of repression of the government. But most people would pay a writer to write for them, popular games were chess or gambling.

Body

(Narrator)

While disease and parasite called the Black-Death consumed the Swedish German population. The local church that would later evolve into a modern civilization Mennonite church a Bishop appointed eighteen soldiers to kill humans with the disease and parasite called the Black Death and to burn or bury them. Before the bishop appointed the eighteen soldiers twelve of them being short range soldiers and six of them long ranged archers, the leader of the soldiers exclaimed he needed a guide. So the leader requested a Monk the Bishop agreeing and sending them with a monk so the journey begins. The eighteen soldiers and monk heading to a near by village briefly talking amongst each other only stopping for rest and sleep. While they were traveling the leader of the men briefly went Mad (Insane) screaming (Leader) "fuck ass shit" (Narrator) and then announcing two of his men two (Leader) "disarm one of the short range soldiers," (Narrator) after disarming the soldier the leader (Leader) "stabbed him in his stomach" (Narrator) every body thinking the man was dead and them burying him, little did they know he went into a slight coma and awoke later. Meanwhile as the men were traveling to the village the men and Monk except the leader, talking and commenting of (Men and Monk) "how you going to do me" when you going to do me"(Narrator) seemingly going crazy the men at first sleeping near the leader all awaking from bad dreams of what they previously were talking and commenting of (Men and Monk) Dreaming "how you going to do me" "when you going to do me." (Narrator) From then after the men sleep at a near and safe distance from the leader, the men awake the second morning. The men noticing a large number of thefts ready to ambush them the only one injured was an archer. The men killing all the thefts even the one who almost stole the leader horse the theft stealing the horse was stabbed to death with the leader's sword as a result of the leader (Leader) "throwing it." (Narrator) The archer that was injured was thought to be dead and buried, little did the men know the archer was not dead he went in to a coma and awoke later. The now sixteen men and monk still traveling reach a village five days later leaving behind weapons that couldn't be moved thru water. All the men and monk arriving at the village the men and monk stopping for food and wine, not knowing that they were drugged and all fell (Men and Monk) "a sleep." All men and monk awoke in a holding cell hands bind being accused of bringing death to the village people and each were given a chance to renounce (Village People) "there God" "and be forgiven" (Narrator) except secretly being hung only two renounced (Two Soldiers) "there God" (Narrator) the rest were all tortured while they were torching the men. The Queen of the village dropped (Queen) "a knife near the holding cell," Narrator) the two soldiers still standing obtained the knife and releasing the monk and them selves. Killing most of the village people returning to there families and the Monk returning to being a Monk. Word has it the village was destroyed by next platoon of men in fact that what happened.

Ending

(Narrator)

The disease and parasite would vanish years and years later. The two remanding soldiers returning to there family's growing old. The monk returned to being a monk, the Swedish human population would flourish eventually.

Writer Anthony Medina
Writer Anthony Richard Medina
Writer Anthony Richard Old English (Dick) Medina Arabic (Holy City)

The Legend of
The Four Brothers

A Short Story

(Narrator)

Once upon a time there were four Brothers unlike any other four Brothers. The oldest of the Brothers stud up in his early twenties and fate took him away. The second oldest Brother the most clever and smartest of all the brothers hid so that fate would not find him. The third oldest of Brothers stud up in his early twenties and fate went over to him and took him away. The youngest of the Brothers was not old enough to be taken away by fate but fate knowing that said I'll return another day. So the second oldest of the Brothers finally stud up in his early twenties holding (Second Oldest Brother) "a sword" (Narrator) and fate appeared to him holding (Fate) "a sword as well." (Narrator) So Brother said (Second Oldest Brother) "I'll challenge you to a fight and not just any fight, so he exclaimed if you can answer a riddle, I'll go with you, if not maybe I'll see you another day, fate said (Fate) "sure." He exclaimed again. Second Oldest Brother) "There are two hemispheres two a brain a right hemisphere and a left hemisphere, a long term memory and a short term memory, neither one can live without the other although, there are studies that show losing one the side that is lost can repair it self, if you take one away what is left zero, one, two, three, or four? Fate said (Fate) "I don't know." (Narrator) So he exclaimed once more (Second Oldest Brother) "the answer is it's a trick question there is no answer." (Narrator) So fate said (Fate) "perhaps I'll see you another day or perhaps not" (Narrator) then fate left. So he exclaimed his final time to the youngest of all Brothers (Second Oldest Brother) fate and destiny is what you make of it, not that you'll ever know, and fate will be there for you someday or perhaps not."

The end

Writer Anthony Medina
Writer Anthony Richard Medina
Writer Anthony Richard Old English (Dick) Medina Arabic (Holy City)

The Book of Evolutions

Non fiction

Evolution first let start off with what is Evolution? An ape turning to a human, but what do all things do throw Evolution? They change (change) Evolution means to change or change but only in a positive way and or path. Let's go to human evolution, a boy that evolves into a Man then a girl that evolves into a Woman. When humans evolved into humans we as a human race started off with a similar color? And also speaking the same language Hebrew but Hebrew back then was very similar to the way Spanish is spoken. How Spanish varies from which country you're in the dialect is different but the language is the same. So Hebrew in America (Turtle Island) would be much different from Hebrew in the Middle East, or German Hebrew would be different from Jewish Hebrew, mainly because elements contribute to the change in dialect of Hebrew. You know the climate is much different in The United States of North America in South America. So African climate is much different from India's climate? Seattle Washington has a lot more rain then Pennsylvania. There for proving how the dialect of Hebrew was and is different? But what I was getting to was and is African people didn't start off brown and with wide nose's it took millions and millions of years to of evolved into there current form? Now it's not all African peoples fault but in some ways and or paths it is? Because, there was always problems since humans evolved. But it took millions and millions of years of negligence to of evolved brown, African people evolving to the shade of brown. You know the sun being harder to shine throw there bodies, forcing there noses to become wider for more oxygen, now humans evolve in more ways then one? Examples not knowing how to read and write, evolving to being able to read and write, next phase a seed evolving to a plant, or like weeds starting off dieing when weed killers are used Weeds evolving into being immune to weed killers. I think in some cases ape did evolve into human but it's a rare case's. Or a puppy evolving into a dog or, a kitten evolving into a cat, or just a animal evolving into a different being. Homosexuals do not evolve they were either born that way or manipulated into that way of life Homosexual are an illness disease parasite pestilence and a plague and a disease needs to be controlled by medicine anti-psychotics depressions medicine and a psychologist and going to a local church and if problem is not fixed being put in a secure prison for consecutive life sentences although I don't think that will help but if anyone is willing to try? Usual evolution is when something evolves to a smarter stronger faster more capable being animals evolve in more ways then one to from an untrained animal or maybe smart or naive to a trained animal. Now I don't have enough time and necessities to tell you of more of evolution but I'm sure you get the idea my theory hold well with most capable being and not all.

The Book of Theories

The Book of Theories

Statement

It is my theory that sex feels better for women?
I assume that sex feels better for women then it does for men? Look at the whole psychologies of it. Women get pregnant? Women have easy excess to custody? Women have easy excess to child support? Women have more organisms then men? If a woman married women have excess to divorce? Women have excess to spousal support? Women have excess to alimony? Women have excess to palimony? Women have easy excess to sex? After a woman is pregnant they stop having a period? Some women after being pregnant don't have to work? Now that theory holds well for most able body women?

Statement

It is to my theory that smokeless tobacco and or chewing tobacco is less harmful for women?
I assume that smokeless tobacco and or chewing tobacco is less harmful for women? Sure smokeless tobacco and or chewing tobacco will inevitably destroy teeth and gums but it is absorbed into a women's body as if they are immune to it? Women are more immune because a women usually is somewhere around half the size of a man? That and women are usually more sophisticated then men because of hygiene? My theory holds well for most able body women and not all?
It is to my theory that woman are more likely to being anemic?
Women have a monthly day long period which results in a loss of blood! Which is how and or the reason for there being more susceptible to being anemic? Treatment for woman should be an Iron pill, milk,

or lactose milk, or 2 percent milk, or 1 percent milk, or soy milk, or coconut milk, or almond milk, peanut butter, or some form of nuts, and a rare cooked piece of meat, and or sushi pre-cooked, and light fruits and vegetables this is treatment for pain, craps, bloating, stress, anxiety as well woman should not work day of period they will be given a day of leave, its is possible that a women being burnt, snipped, and twisted, and fixed, can result in no period for women? Or women periodic period should end at age forty five? Working more days before is how work is made up! Do not take any substance if allergic or have medical condition!

Statement

It is to my theory that women are more likely to being and or having Bi-polar and or Anxiety?

I assume that women are more likely to being and or having bi-polar and or anxiety? Sure it is possible for a woman to make choices and or decisions base off of intellectual ability? But more often then not a woman makes judgment based off of feelings? Women are very similar to cats because of there intelligence, curiosity, playfulness? Women usually have lots of opinions, question, advice, suggestions, input, and ideas? Usually speaking women are very manipulative? Usually speaking women communicate and or talk a-lot? Not always but usually women from kindergarten through twelfth grade women have higher scores in Social Studies, English, Communication Arts, Language, and Math? That and women are more immune to taking Anxiety medication because women metabolize anxiety medication better then men do? Just because women are more immune to anxiety medicine doesn't make anxiety medicine healthy? That and women have a higher tolerance to drugs then men do? Women can hold there breath longer then men can? Women are more sophisticated then men because of hygiene which is the reason that anxiety medication is less harmful for them? My theory holds well for most able body women and not all?

Statement

It is to my theory that women are truly the sixth scent?

I assume that women truly are the sixth scent? It is possible for a women to make choices and or decisions based off of intellectual abilities, but more often then not women make judgment based off of feelings, and who's to say that's wrong it is possible that there is truth to that and maybe some would say there's no truth behind that but which explains the reason women are truly the sixth scent? Women just need to express themselves in a positive way? Women have a lot of opinions, questions, advice, suggestions, input and ideas? Women are very similar to cats because of intelligence, curiosity, and playfulness? Usually women are very manipulative? Women are more sophisticated then men because of hygiene? My theory holds well for most able body women and not all?

Statement

It is my theory that disease can bring a dead human back to life?

If a person is inches from there last breath? Putting a disease in them will create cells for oxygen? Also reanimating there genes and bringing them back to life? Disease can be put into a body two ways either in thru the eyes or in thru the mouth? Now that theory holds well for an able body person inches from there last breath? My theory is less if the person is dieing from old age? My theory is less if the body is dieing from a current disease? My theory is negative if the body has only half a body? My theory is less if a body is mortally wounded? My theory holds well for most able body humans and not all? My theory holds well but the disease with kill you inevitable?

Statement

It is my theory that disease can bring a dead animal back to life?

If an animal is inches from there last breath? Putting a disease into them will create cells for oxygen? Also reanimating there genes and bringing them back to life? Disease can be introduced either thru the eyes or in thru the mouth? Now my theory holds well for an able body animal inches from there last breath? My theory is less if an animal is dieing from old age? My theory is less is an animal is dieing from a current disease? My theory is negative if an animal only has half a body? My theory is less if an animal is mortally wounded? My theory holds well for most able body animals and not all? My theory holds well but a disease will kill you inevitable?

Statement

It is my theory that introducing a disease. Into a humans body while having a heart attack can postpone a heart attack?

A disease can be introduced into a body either in the eyes or in the mouth? The reason a disease can postpone a heart attack? Is because a disease will kill you inevitable? But a disease will make your body shut down slowly? Or a disease will make your body slow down? The likeliness of this working is slight because of time? My theory holds well for most able body people and not all?

Statement

It is my theory that cleaning, stressing exercising, drinking tea, dieting, prayer or meditation, can reduce symptoms of mental illness?

Cleaning can reduce symptom of mental illness because the cleaner you are the healthier you are? Stressing can reduce symptoms of mental illness because the healthier you are is the happier you are? Exercising can reduce symptoms of mental illness because? The healthier you are is the happier you are? Drinking tea can reduce symptoms of stress and or anxiety? Diet is important for proper brain function? Prayer or meditation is good for relaxing? Now this theory holds well for most able body people and no exceptions? My theory is negative for diagnose, treating, curing illness? My theory holds well as a supplement?

Statement

It is my theory that cleaning, stressing, exercising, drinking tea, dieting, prayer or meditation, can reduce stress?

Cleaning can reduce stress? Because the cleaner you are the happier you are? Stressing can reduce stress because the healthier you are the happier you are? Exercising can reduce stress because the healthier you are the happier you are? Drinking tea can reduce stress or anxiety? Diet is important for proper brain function? Prayer or meditation is good for relaxing? My theory holds well for most able body humans and not all? My theory holds well for if practiced regularly? My theory is negative for curing, treating, diagnosing, Illness?

Statement

It is my theory that weeds are evolved to being immune to weed killers? Every time someone puts weed killer over weeds I notice that the weed killer doesn't kill the weeds? It drowns the weeds like putting to much water in a plant? Weeds thru time have build up a tolerance to weed killer? Like a person building a tolerance to drugs? Another thing why do weeds grow back after weed killer has been put over them it's because the weed killer didn't kill the weed it drowned it? My theory hold well for most weeds not all? The best thing to eliminate a weed is by pulling the roots out of the ground and putting weed eater over that spot? My theory holds well for most able body weeds and not all?

Statement

It is my theory that coma clients should be treated with? In thee event of a coma followed by prescribed medication I will be dieted once a day with fish not shell fish, fruits, vegetables, water and a diet of healthy food and drink? And I will be given a fish oil pill? I will undergo a monitor, panels, morphine one hour a day alternatives to Morphine pain relieving medication vitamins one hour a day adrenaline one hour a day? Head straps body straps arm straps leg straps and a neck brace that can be removed if needed? Only international countries and me Anthony Medina I will undergo a lie detector as form of communication? Serialize and sanitize equipment and accessories before use? And radio one hour a day nothing that has parental advisory? Television one hour a day nothing above a pg thirteen rating? visitation of relatives one hour a day? Hospital security patrolling area regularly? A Pastor lecturing a sermon or religious television a half hour Sundays? Sunroom one hour a day? Chiropractor one hour a day? I will have eye coverings? I will have sunglasses? And my hygienic and oral health will be taken care of regularly? As well as my surrounding cleaning needs regularly? The reason I will undergo a trial of this sort is to reverse the effects of a coma?

Statement

It is my theory that Alzheimer clients should be treated with?

In thee event of Alzheimer followed by prescribed medication? I will be given a fish oil pill, and an iron pill, a vitamin c pill, a vitamin e pill, a vitamin b pill? And I will be dieted with fish not shell fish, fruits, vegetables, water, and I will be feed that once a day? And I will practice writing and reading? I will have excellent oral hygienic health and excellent hygienic health as well? The reason I will undergo a trial of this sort so that I may reverse effects of Alzheimer?

Statement

It is my theory that cancer clients should be treated with?

In thee event of cancer followed by prescribed medication and light chemo therapy, I will be advised and undergo lung transplants regarding cancer, and advised and undergo a operation regarding cancer, I will exercise regularly, and be dieted with healthy food and drink, and be given a iron pill, a vitamin c pill, a vitamin e pill, a vitamin b pill, a fish oil pill. I will have excellent oral hygienic health and excellent hygienic health as well. The reason I will undergo a trial of this sort is to reverse the effects of cancer.

Writer Anthony Richard Old English (Dick) Medina Arabic (Holy City)
Writer Anthony Richard Medina
Writer Anthony Medina

Notes

Notes

Writer Anthony Medina

Phone (717) 847-4506

Mailing Address

Anthony Medina
155 East Park Street Apt 309
Elizabethtown Pa 17022

Printed in the United States
By Bookmasters